Flea Biscuit's Magic Christmas

Matthew Bonazzoli

To all of the fans who were inspired by these books to send me pictures, drawings and stories of their own. You have made my life richer.

Contents

Acknowledgements

Thank you to my sister Laura for editing, to Jim Odo for the wonderful illustrations, to my wife, Maria for helping me rescue so many animals, and to everyone who enjoyed the first two books and encouraged me to complete the series.

Chapter 1

Fire and Ice

Shortly after bedtime Flea Biscuit awoke to a loud, piercing whine. The sound made his fur tingle like the charge he sometimes gets from the blankets. The little girl quickly sat up and switched on the lamp by the bed. She looked afraid. Something must be wrong. The bedroom door swung open and the woman came into the room dressed in her night-robe. Thick black smoke rolled in across the ceiling. The woman grabbed a blanket, wrapped Flea Biscuit up to his neck, took the little girl's hand, and led her quickly out of the room.

The hall was filled with smoke so thick it was difficult to see. They all began coughing as they struggled down the hall and into the living room. Flea Biscuit squirmed in his blanket, for he was very afraid, but his legs were wrapped tightly and he could not move. Then suddenly there was a loud *BANG!* and the lights went out. In the darkness, Flea Biscuit saw an orange glow approaching from the back of the house. The woman clutched him even more tightly as she felt her way to the front door. She tucked Flea Biscuit under her arm and fought to get the door open. The little tiger continued to twist and turn in the blanket, now in a panic. At last, the door flew open and they rushed out into the cold night air. They slipped and slid on the icy driveway as they ran away from the house.

When they had reached a safe distance, Flea Biscuit looked back. Over the woman's shoulder, he could see flames surging across the roof of their home. "What has happened?" he cried.

The woman unwrapped Flea Biscuit and handed him to the little girl, instructing her to hold him tightly. Then she wrapped the little girl in the blanket and told her not to move from that spot. Soon came the sound of sirens growing louder and louder. Large red trucks arrived with big bright lights. Men in heavy suits jumped out and began pulling something that looked like a long snake out of the side of the trucks. It was all so terrifying and confusing to Flea Biscuit. The little girl pulled a small corner of the blanket over his head but it did not cover his face. Wide eyed, he howled in terror as he saw the flames engulf his home.

The men began spraying water on the house, but the wind whipped the flames high into the air. Terrible black smoke filled the sky as if racing to hide the stars. The little girl began to cry. Flea Biscuit tried to bury his head beneath her chin, but she was shivering so hard her head and shoulders shook. Then a man dressed in one of the heavy suits came and wrapped a large blanket around them both. He took them to a car and let them sit inside. Soon, the woman joined them in the back seat. They sat in the warm car together and watched as their home collapsed into the flames.

"My home!" Flea Biscuit cried. "My home!"

Chapter 2

A Cold Winter

Spike squinted as the winter wind rushed through his fur and blew his whiskers back. He was sitting on the back porch by a dish of food, waiting for his friend the possum to show up for dinner. "Maybe it's too cold tonight," he thought as he stared into the clear sky. A bright star hung high above the trees. Winter had come early this year. The leaves on the trees were still changing colors when the first freeze had descended upon the big old house. Cheeto had since become content to spend his nights curled up on the cat bed by the fireplace, but Spike, as always, was restless.

Although he loved the quiet solitude of the cold nights, the sting of the frozen wind on his ears brought to his mind the hardships of his days trying to survive in the woods as a field cat. Perhaps that was the reason for his unlikely friendship with the possum. It connected him back to his days in the wild before the man had brought him to this house.

The door slid open behind Spike as the man let Cheeto outside. The orange tabby shivered a bit. "Brrrrr! It's so cold tonight!" he said. He waited, but Spike did not reply. He spoke again. "Are you still waiting for him?"

Again, Spike did not answer. He just sat still, braced against the wind, scanning the line of trees for his friend's approach.

Cheeto sat down beside him. They were both quiet for a long time. Then, as the bright star rose even higher in the sky, they heard a short squeak. From behind a large old tree came the possum to eat.

"Ah, here he is," said Cheeto. "And it's high time too. My toes are freezing."

"Think of how cold he must be," said Spike.

"Aye, let's hope he's better at growing a winter coat than I am."

The possum stuck his nose into the bowl and began to crunch on the food. Spike guarded the porch. His eyes moved left and right among the trees. Occasionally, the possum would glance up at Spike for assurance that he was watching over him.

With a final crunch, the possum lifted his head. He looked up at Spike as if he were going to speak, but did not. Spike looked down at his friend and slowly blinked. Finally, the possum squeaked, then turned and headed back to the woods.

"Have a good night, Laddie!" Cheeto called out. The possum let out another faint squeak in return.

The wind was whipping now, and it pulled on the cats' whiskers. Cheeto turned to Spike. "Well, will you come back inside now?"

"Yes," said Spike. He turned towards the sliding glass door, but paused to watch as the possum trudged through the cold back to his den in the forest. He noticed that his friend looked very old. "Then again," he thought, "possums always do look very young or very old. If this is to be his last season, I hope he is comfortable."

Spike's thoughts were interrupted by the sound of a car pulling up to the front of the house.

"Well, who could that be at this hour on such a cold night?" asked Cheeto.

"Yes, odd," replied Spike.

The two cats hopped off the porch and went around to the front of the house to see who had arrived.

Chapter 3

An Unhappy Reunion

On the front porch, Spike and Cheeto saw the woman, the little girl, and Flea Biscuit, all wrapped in blankets, shivering in the cold. The man quickly opened the door and welcomed them inside. Spike and Cheeto followed closely behind, knowing that something unfortunate must have happened. The man took them to warm up by the fireplace. As the woman began to speak, the little girl lowered Flea Biscuit down to the floor. The moment he was free, he ran under the nearby couch and began to cry.

Cheeto poked his head under the couch and said to Flea Biscuit, "Now, now, Laddie, it can't be as bad as all that. Come out and tell me all about it."

Flea Biscuit simply buried his face into the corner and continued to cry.

Cheeto squeezed himself under the couch and tried again to comfort Flea Biscuit. It was no use. After several minutes, he gave up and came back out.

"What has happened?" asked Spike.

"I don't know," replied Cheeto. "The laddie won't tell me a thing. He just sits under there crying. He's had an awful scare, though, I'll tell you that, and he smells of smoke."

"Is he injured?" Spike asked.

Cheeto thought a moment. "I don't know. I don't think so, but he won't let me get close enough to see."

The little girl and the woman were crying, too. The man did his best to console them.

"Oh, this is terrible," lamented Cheeto. "Whatever shall we do?"

"We cannot solve the problems of humans," said Spike, "so we'd best focus on the house cat."

"Aye," Cheeto agreed. "I'll give it another go and see if he'll come out."

Chapter 4

The Knights Order of the Cats

It was now well past midnight. The man had made a place to sleep in the spare rooms for the woman and the little girl. Outside, the cold wind howled like a lonely ghost searching for refuge. Inside, though, the house was quiet and warm.

The fireplace began to darken as the last of the wood burned down. Beneath the couch, Flea Biscuit was still hiding.

Cheeto was becoming distraught. "I've tried everything! He will not come out, nor will he tell me what happened. All he'll say is something about his home being gone."

"Gone?" asked Spike, surprised. "What trouble has he gotten himself into now?" He shook his head. "Well, I expect he'll come out in the morning when he gets hungry enough." He turned and began to walk away.

"Spike!" scolded Cheeto. "That's not how you treat a friend in need!"

Spike considered this a moment, groaned softly, then returned to the couch.

Cheeto squeezed back under and called to Flea Biscuit. Again, the little tiger did not move. He just shook with fear.

After a few seconds, Spike peered under the couch at Cheeto. "No luck?"

Cheeto shook his head. He crawled back out. "Well, this is just very sad and you're no help at all," he said.

Spike sighed, then poked his head under the couch. In a booming voice he commanded, "By the Knights Order of the Cats it is decreed that Flea

Biscuit be made an official member of this household. Come sit and be counted now or forgo the honor forever!"

Spike pulled his head from under the couch and sat beside Cheeto, who was staring at him with a look of confusion on his face. "What are you doing?" he whispered. "There is no Knights Order of the Cats!"

"There is now," Spike said.

Slowly Flea Biscuit's head poked out from under the couch. His face was wet with tears. "I am here to be counted, Sir."

"Ah, good," said Cheeto, joining in with the most dignified voice he could muster. "Ahem—uhm—sit and be knighted." As Flea Biscuit crawled out from under the couch, Cheeto leaned toward Spike and whispered, "What do we do now?"

Flea Biscuit sniffled as he sat beside Cheeto. Spike stood facing him. He put his right paw on top of Flea Biscuit's head and decreed, "I dub you Flea Biscuit of the Order of Knighted Cats."

"Knights Order of the Cats," corrected Cheeto.

Spike stuttered. "Yes, that."

This was getting to be fun, thought Cheeto. "Now raise your right paw," he said.

Flea Biscuit puffed out his chest and raised his paw as instructed. It seemed that the ceremony was distracting him from his worries.

"Do you swear to maintain the honor of the cats of this household and all cats both wild and domesticated?" asked Spike in a booming voice.

"I do!" answered Flea Biscuit in the most confident voice he could muster.

"You are so knighted," said Spike. "And may you never forget this solemn oath."

"Welcome to the club, Flea Biscuit," said Cheeto as he patted him on the shoulder. "Now, will you tell us what has happened to you this night?"

Until dawn, Flea Biscuit recounted his story. Each time he told it, he became a little less confused. Having his friends there to listen helped him calm down and gave him hope that maybe things would soon be all right.

Chapter 5

Breakfast

Cheeto slowly opened his eyes and sniffed the air. The unfamiliar smell of bacon and eggs was wafting from the kitchen. "My word! What is that delightfully tasty dish being cooked?" he wondered. His stomach rumbling, he headed for the kitchen. The woman was standing at the stove making breakfast. Flea Biscuit was waiting by her feet looking up at her. At the table sat the little girl.

"Little one, what is she cooking?" Cheeto asked.

"Breakfast," was all Flea Biscuit replied.

"Can I have some?" Cheeto asked.

Flea Biscuit shook his head. "She doesn't make it for us, but I keep hoping she'll give me a taste."

Cheeto sat beside Flea Biscuit and imitated him by looking up at the woman. "The man never cooks much at all and he certainly never makes anything that smells this tasty," he said.

The woman put food on a plate and placed it on the table for the little girl to eat. The man came downstairs and sat down at the table with the little girl. He gave her a smile and tapped her on the nose. She giggled.

The woman set two more plates onto the table, then sat down to eat.

"Well, why don't we get some?" asked Cheeto.

"That is human food!" said Spike as he walked into the kitchen. "Be grateful for your own meals."

Flea Biscuit and Cheeto ignored Spike, moved closer to the table, and began staring up at the humans longingly.

"Beggars!" said Spike. His voice was disdainful, but in truth the smell was beginning to make him very curious and hungry himself. He walked past the other cats, went directly to the feet of the little girl, and tapped her on the leg. She giggled, reached down, and gave Spike a small piece of bacon. Spike took it and walked out of the kitchen, his claws tapping confidently on the floor as he went.

As Flea Biscuit and Cheeto watched this, their mouths hung open. Both were about to try the same thing when the woman

scolded the little girl for sharing her food with the cats. It seemed they would need to be content with just smelling the food.

"Come, Laddie,"said Cheeto. "Just the smell of it will make our own breakfast taste better." He paused and then added, "Remind me later to ask Spike what it tasted like."

Chapter 6

Beneath the Silver Sky

Spike went outside to scout for prey around the house and get some exercise, but Cheeto decided to stay in with his little friend. Flea Biscuit had been through quite a lot the previous night and he thought he could do more good by offering companionship than by hunting.

Beneath a silver winter sky, Spike circled around the perimeter of the house several times looking for signs of prey. There was nothing. He then climbed a tree in the yard to watch from above. He was careful to position himself where his black fur would absorb the warmth of the limited sunlight. It was a very cold day. "It feels like it will snow tonight," he thought. Spike squinted and scanned the yard for any motion.

Suddenly, his attention was drawn to movement by the tree line. To his dismay, it was not prey, but a golden brown dog scampering in and out along the edge of the forest. Abby was out with her master, the old farmer. It seemed Spike was not the only one willing to hunt outside on such a frigid day. He admired Abby and the farmer for their work ethic and hoped that they were having better luck than he was.

Spotting Spike in the tree, Abby trotted over. "You're not very good at hiding up there," she said. "I could spot your black fur shining in the sun from way back in the forest. Would you like to play chase with me?"

"No, I would not like to play chase with you," Spike replied. He was annoyed. "Go away. You'll spoil my chances of catching something."

"Oh, we've already caught plenty," Abby said excitedly. "Two of the largest birds you ever saw. My master is going to give one to your man."

This was something Spike needed to see to believe. He had never heard of humans hunting a bird. "Why would they do that?" he wondered, but as the old farmer approached, he understood. Draped over the man's shoulder were two birds far larger than he had ever seen. Twice the size of any cat and nearly the size of Abby. Spike was bewildered.

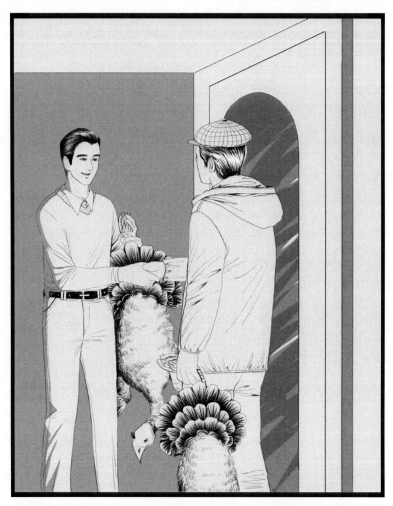

"They are called turkeys," said Abby with a sense of superiority. "A cat like you could never hunt them but my master and I can."

Spike stared at the birds, wondering what it would be like to hunt for such large prey. He would certainly be proud to catch one of those and bring it to the house for the man to make into sandwiches.

The old farmer knocked on the door. The man came out onto the porch. He graciously accepted one of the turkeys and shook the farmer's hand in thanks. Then the farmer whistled and Abby jumped on two legs to turn and run to him. "Well, I'll see you later, Spike. Next time maybe we will play chase! I hope your human enjoys the turkey."

Spike, still marveling at the large bird, simply nodded and said, "Thank you," as Abby ran back towards her master and home.

Chapter 7

Four's a Crowd

Flea Biscuit and Cheeto curled up on the couch with the little girl. She seemed upset and tired. The two cats hoped they could give her some comfort.

The man got a blanket and draped it over the little girl. Then he gave a coat to the woman and helped her put it on. He told the little girl they had to leave to take care of a few things, but would be back soon. When he opened the door to leave, Spike slinked back inside. He had had enough of the cold for one day.

As soon as the door closed and the man and the woman were gone, the little girl buried her face in the pillow and began to cry loudly. Flea Biscuit and Cheeto tried to console her, but she just pulled up the blanket and cried even louder.

Spike came in the room. "What is that horrible noise?" he howled. He saw that it was the little girl on the couch. "Stop that!" he howled, but she continued.

"She's still very upset, Spike," said Cheeto. "What should we do?"

Flea Biscuit gently licked the little girl's face.

"Well, this will do no good but to drive me mad," Spike responded, "and you two know better than to be on the furniture!" Spike walked over to the little girl, reached up, and swatted at her leg beneath the blanket. "Stop that!" he demanded. "Do you hear? I said, stop that noise!" He swatted her leg again.   The little girl stopped crying, sat up and wiped the tears from her face.

"That's better," said Spike as he turned to leave the room. He did not get more than two steps away when he was suddenly scooped up into the little girl's arms and deposited on the sofa beside Flea Biscuit and

Cheeto. "Let go of me!" He howled and squirmed, but she held him tight. "I have claws!" he protested. "I'll use them even if you are a child!"

Cheeto thought this was all very amusing. "Now Spike, she's upset. Do your best and don't upset her further or she'll cry again."

At this, Spike resolved to stay still at least until she fell asleep. The little girl relaxed a bit on the pillow with her arms around Spike.

"Don't you know better than to be on the furniture, Spike?" joked Flea Biscuit.

Cheeto and Flea Biscuit began to laugh at how uncomfortable Spike looked. Spike tried to swat at the little tiger's head, but he was being held too tightly to move. The little girl giggled and closed her eyes. After a while she did fall asleep, as did Flea Biscuit and Cheeto. Spike just sighed and stared up at the dust on the ceiling light. Eventually, he was able to ease himself out from under her arms. As he slid off the sofa, he realized that helping the little girl fall asleep had given him an odd feeling of comfort. Before leaving the room, he stopped to look again at the little girl on the couch, and then at Cheeto and Flea Biscuit snoozing away. "House cats," he said quietly as he rolled his eyes.

Chapter 8

The First Snow

The man and woman arrived back at the big old house just before dark. They were carrying boxes and bags filled with new clothes and other things for the girl and the woman. In one of the bags, the little girl found a stick that had a string with a bright feather tied to it. She began waving the stick in front of Flea Biscuit and Cheeto. They chased after the feather, reaching out and trying to catch it, but just as they did she would pull it away. They were having great fun. The woman knelt down and gave the girl a big hug while the man went to the fireplace and began to light it. It was going to be another cold night and the first snowfall of the winter had already begun.

As soon as he saw the flames, Flea Biscuit stopped playing. He stood and stared at the fire.

Cheeto tried to assure him it was all right. "Now, Laddie, fire can be good or bad like anything else," he said. "The man knows perfectly well what he's doing and besides, think of how nice it feels on a cold night." At this, the orange tabby jumped up into the bed by the fireplace to show Flea Biscuit that there was nothing to be afraid of.

The little tiger considered what his friend had said and, after some hesitation, decided to trust him. When the fire was burning well, he hopped into the bed with Cheeto so they could absorb the warmth together.

After leaving some food out for the possum, the man sat with the woman and little girl on the couch. The woman read a book to the girl while the man studied some papers.

"What do you think will happen to me and my humans?" asked Flea Biscuit. "I have lost my forever home and I fear that I will be sent away." The little cat began to cry again at the thought of being separated from his family.

Cheeto sat straight up and looked at the little tiger, "Now, Laddie, do you not know that a forever home is not some building that can be taken away or destroyed?"

"It's not?" questioned the little tiger.

"Why, no! Of course it isn't." Cheeto continued. "Your forever home is with friends, family, and the people who love you. It can be anywhere at all, and right now, the home for you and your humans is here."

"But what will we do?" implored Flea Biscuit. "Eventually we will need to leave."

Cheeto considered this quietly, then answered, "Laddie, legend has it that this time of year is magical and all sorts of wishes can be granted if you only believe strongly enough."

"Really?" said Flea Biscuit earnestly. "Do you think it's true?"

Cheeto paused again as if deep in thought, then replied, "In my life, I have seen things I thought were as real as you and me turn out to be nothing but fables. And I have seen many wondrous things happen that I never thought were possible. All of us being together and safe on this snowy winter night is a blessing in itself. Now, I have heard that the humans also believe that this is a magical time of year, though I don't know for sure. I do know that the man cares very much for you, the little girl, and her mother."

"How do you know?" asked the little tiger.

"Well, because the woman comes here quite often and she and the man seem to enjoy each other's company very much."

Flea Biscuit was surprised to hear this. "How did I not know this?" he wondered. "She comes here without me?" he asked.

"Well yes, of course. Humans do many things without bringing their cats along," Cheeto laughed. "Now let's have a nap and do not worry about a thing. It will all be okay."

Flea Biscuit put his head down. He was tired from all of the playing earlier, but before he drifted off to sleep, he decided that he would wish really hard for everything to be well with his friends and family. As he wished for happy times, his eyelids grew heavy and eventually he fell asleep.

Through the sliding glass door in the kitchen, Spike looked out to the back porch, watching as the possum quickly ate his meal before the food became covered in snow. Spike tapped the window to let the possum know he was there and keeping watch. His friend finished eating, gave Spike a grateful squeak, and then turned to trudge back to his den deep in the forest. Spike felt very sad for the hardships of the wild beasts and hoped that his friend would fare well through this storm. From where he sat, safe and warm in the house, the snow looked beautiful as it fell, but he knew that for some creatures this would be a difficult night.

Chapter 9

Digging Out

Early in the morning, the man put on his heavy coat, went outside, and began to shovel the snow that covered the driveway. He then cleared the snow from the front and back porches and down to the road. Spike sat on the porch keeping the man company as he worked. When the man was finished, he shook the snow off his coat, and he and the black cat walked back into the house. The woman was in the kitchen making breakfast for everyone. As she called out to the little girl to come down to eat, she almost tripped over Flea Biscuit and Cheeto, who were at her feet again hoping for a taste.

The woman reached down and picked up Cheeto. This surprised him very much. She gave him a hug and a few pats on the head before putting him down and returning to her cooking.

"I think she likes you," said Flea Biscuit.

Cheeto nodded, grateful for the woman's attention. He began to rub against her leg, but was then distracted by the smell of bacon again. He turned to Flea Biscuit. "She does this every morning?" asked Cheeto.

"Pretty much, yes," said Flea Biscuit.

Cheeto inhaled the strong, tasty scent deeply. "Your humans are wonderful," he said. "I may just want to move in with you once you're all settled again."

Flea Biscuit began to laugh, but the thought of having to leave his friends again also made him feel sad.

From behind them came Spike. "Well, it would be nice to have this house to myself again. There's always so much noise now and so much going on. I can't relax."

"Oh, Spike," said Cheeto, "you've always slept with one eye open." Cheeto giggled and went over to sit at the feet of the little girl as she ate, futilely hoping that today she'd let him have a bite.

As they finished their breakfast, the cats heard the sounds of a dog barking urgently. "That's Abby," said Cheeto, "and she sounds very upset."

The man went to the front door to see what was happening. Abby was standing in front of the house, barking insistently. The man went outside and Cheeto and Spike followed him to the front porch.

Still barking, Abby began to jump up at the man.

"What has happened?" asked Spike. "Where is your human?"

Abby continued to jump at the man. "My master has fallen down," she cried. "We were out shoveling the snow when he suddenly fell down and I could not get him to move!"

With a look of concern on his face, the man went inside to get his coat. He returned with an old rope, looped it onto Abby's collar, and began to walk her back to the farmhouse.

The two cats tried to hop through the snow to follow, but the man turned and scolded them to get back to the house. Cheeto turned back at once, but Spike, his black fur a stark contrast against the snow, stood defiantly glaring at the man.

"Come back to the house," called Cheeto, but Spike refused to move. "Spike," said Cheeto, "the man has enough to do now without worrying about you freezing in the snow."

Spike snapped back, "I would not freeze in the snow!" Nevertheless, he relented and turned around to go back into the house with Cheeto.

Abby pulled on the rope, leading the man as quickly as she could to the farmhouse. As they approached, and she saw her master lying in the snow beside his shovel, she broke free and ran to his side. She nudged his body, whimpering and howling, but he didn't move. The man knelt beside him for a moment, then went into the farmhouse. He came back with some blankets and covered the body. Then he led Abby to the farmhouse steps and sat with his arm around her until a white truck with flashing red lights arrived

Chapter 10

A Sad Day for Abby

The sun was setting by the time the man returned home. He brought Abby back with him. The three cats watched as the woman gave him a hug and he unhooked the dog from her leash. They could see that Abby was not her usual energetic self. Instead, she simply lay down at the man's feet and whimpered.

Spike was the first to speak. "Will your human be all right?" he asked.

Abby sighed. "My master is gone. I will miss him so much. He was a good human and now I will never get to play tag or chase with him again."

"What will happen?" asked Flea Biscuit.

Abby sat up a bit and said, "My master's sister will come. She does not like me. She has three poodles, which are worse than cats." Abby realized what she'd said and added, "No offense to you."

Spike just rolled his eyes.

"None taken, friend," said Cheeto in a comforting voice.

Abby continued, "Surely she will send me off to a shelter. I was in a shelter when I was a puppy before my master adopted me. They will put me alone in a cage unless another human wants to adopt me, but it is winter and people have other concerns than dogs after the snow begins to fall."

"Oh, this is terrible," said Flea Biscuit. He looked at Cheeto and angrily said, "You told me this was a magical time of year and wishes can come true, but I wished all last night for good things and now Abby has lost her human! You lied to me!" Flea Biscuit turned and ran down the hall.

Spike turned to Cheeto. "You'd best look after the house cat," he said. "I will stay with Abby."

Cheeto's shoulders slumped as he turned to follow Flea Biscuit. In a weary voice, he sighed, "Aye."

"And stop filling his young mind with stories of magic!" Spike added.

The man approached, stroked Abby's head, and led her into the room with the fireplace. She lay by the fire and rested her head on her paws.

Spike followed them into the room, but he did not know what to say to comfort her, so instead he simply sat beside her. As the man kneeled, he poked a metal rod into the embers and let out a heavy sigh. He gently reached down and patted Abby on the head. He then moved his hand towards Spike. At first, Spike raised his paw to swat the man's hand away, but then, he tilted his head into the man's palm. Spike could sense that the man was also upset about the passing of the old farmer and thought that maybe he, too, needed a friend.

Chapter 11

A Friend in Need

Cheeto found Flea Biscuit hiding in the spare bedroom under the little girl's bed. "Come now, little one, crying won't make things any better."

From under the bed came a sad voice. "I don't know what to believe anymore. I have lost my home, Abby has lost her human, and there's nothing we can do to help."

Cheeto thought for a few seconds. He decided the best way to help Flea Biscuit feel better would be to show him a way to help someone else—and right now, Abby needed friends.

"That's not true, Flea Biscuit," he said. "You can help Abby. You can't bring her master back but you can help make her feel welcome in this house. As members of the Knights Order of the Cats, it is our duty to help whosoever here needs us."

A small voice came from beneath the bed. "But you said this was a magic time of year, and only bad things are happening."

"Aye, I did say that, little one, and I believe it, but you need to have faith for the magic to work. Did you think it all just happens on its own? We all need to help the magic along, each and every one of us, and I think right now maybe we can work a little magic of our own for a very sad doggy downstairs. Now I'm going to go and be with our friend. You can stay up here and sulk all you want, but it'll do no good."

Flea Biscuit sat alone in the dark under the bed and thought a lot about what his friend had said. He remembered how Cheeto, and even Spike, had welcomed him the night of the fire. He decided that the orange tabby was right, and he could help Abby feel welcome, too, by being with her.

He went downstairs and into the room with the fireplace. Spike and Cheeto were sitting beside Abby in the glow of the fire.

"Are you okay Abby?" he asked timidly.

Abby looked up at the little tiger with sad eyes, but did not respond.

Flea Biscuit rubbed his cheek against her head.

This time, she spoke. "I have lost my master and my only family. We were a good pack, even though it was just the two of us. A dog needs a pack to live. I don't know…" her words trailed off as she put her head back down.

Cheeto looked down at Abby and then at Spike. He was surprised to see such a look of concern shining in the black cat's green eyes, but Spike said nothing.

Flea Biscuit lay down, pushed up against Abby, and said, "Then we will be your pack until you find another one."

"Yes," said Cheeto who also lay beside Abby.

Spike did not move, but echoed their sentiment with a simple and soft-spoken, "Yes."

Abby licked both Flea Biscuit and Cheeto on their heads. Flea Biscuit giggled and said, "I will play chase with you, too, but this time do not chase me out of the house." Abby's spirits seemed to lift a little at this.

As he walked out of the room, Spike said, "There is no playing chase in the house." He then went to the kitchen to sit by the sliding glass door and watch for his friend the possum to come for his food.

After several minutes, Cheeto sat down beside him. "Has he come yet?" he asked.

"No," answered Spike. "Perhaps it is just too cold tonight for him to leave his den. Or perhaps the snow is too deep and he cannot get out. I don't know."

Cheeto nodded, but said nothing. He could sense that Spike was lost in thoughts of his friend.

After several minutes of silence, Spike nodded towards the room with the fireplace where Flea Biscuit and Abby were resting and asked, "How are they doing in there?"

"They are both sleeping like peas in a pod," said Cheeto. "Everything will be all right, won't it, Spike?" He sounded as if he needed some reassurance.

"Yes," Spike answered, even though he did not know what the future would bring. "Everything will be fine."

Flea Biscuit's Magic Christmas

Chapter 12

Fair Is Fair

The next morning, Flea Biscuit awoke from his spot on the little girl's bed. He had overslept! She was gone and the house was very quiet. He went down the stairs to find his friends.

Cheeto was sitting by the front door. "Little one," he asked, "how are you this morning?"

"I'm worried," said Flea Biscuit. "Where is everyone?"

"Spike went up to the attic to look for mice after the humans left with Abby," replied Cheeto.

Flea Biscuit became concerned for his friend. "Where did they take Abby?"

"I don't know," said Cheeto. "The man put her on a leash and they all left early this morning. It may have been time for her to go to her new owner."

"How could they do that?" Flea Biscuit cried. "How could they just give Abby away?"

"Well, don't hold it against our humans," said Cheeto in a consoling voice. "Abby did not belong to them. She is the property of her master's sister now, and it's up to her what will happen."

"But Abby wanted to stay here. That's not fair!" shouted Flea Biscuit.

Spike was just coming down the stairs. "Fair?" he growled as he walked past them. "Do not expect life to be fair, Flea! If you want the world to be a better place, then you have to help make that happen."

Cheeto frowned. "Spike, right or not, you don't need to be so harsh all the time." He then turned to Flea Biscuit and said in a kind voice, "It's up to each of us to help balance things out and make the world a better place. Have faith in the man. I'm sure he will do what's best for Abby."

Spike huffed and continued walking down the hall. He was heading to the kitchen to look out the sliding glass window. The food from last night sat uneaten and frozen to the bowl. He was worried for his friend, but there was nothing he could do.

"Now, little tiger," said Cheeto, shall we go and sit by one of the windows and watch the winter birds?"

"I would like that," said Flea Biscuit, "but first I would like to eat breakfast."

"Well," said Cheeto, "I have already eaten, but perhaps I can fit in a wee bit more."

As the two cats crunched on their food, Flea Biscuit considered what Spike had said. It occurred to him that every day he witnessed his friends and even the humans working to help each other. "I guess what Spike said is right," he thought. As a member of the Knights Order of the Cats, he had a duty to find ways of making the world a better place for everyone he loved.

Chapter 13

A Tree in the House

From their spot looking out the window at the birds, Flea Biscuit and Cheeto saw the man's car approach up the road through the snow. "Oh no!" exclaimed Flea Biscuit. "It looks like a tree has fallen on the man's car."

"We'd better go and check to be sure everyone is all right," said Cheeto.

They ran to the front door to greet their humans. Spike quickly came to the door so that he could go outside as soon as it opened.

There was a banging sound on the porch and then the door opened and the three humans came in the house carrying a tree!

Spike was so taken aback that he forgot all about going outside and simply stared in disbelief. He had spent several winters with the man, but had never seen him bring a tree into the house.

"A tree in the house!" Cheeto exclaimed. "What's going on now?"

"Maybe it's sick," added Flea Biscuit, "and they're going to help it get better."

"Don't be ridiculous, Flea," said Spike. "The man will make firewood out of it."

"Maybe," said Cheeto, "but he's never cut up a tree in the house before."

They all followed the humans into the room with the fireplace, where the man placed the stump of the tree in a metal base and stood it up in a corner. Then the woman and the little girl brought in several small boxes. The cats sat fascinated by the spectacle as bright shiny balls and silver strings were taken out of the boxes and hung on the tree. Cheeto hoped the humans would empty the boxes so he could sit in one of them.

For hours the humans worked on the tree while the cats watched. Flea Biscuit loved the smell of the freshly cut pine. Still, he missed Abby. "Do you think the humans traded Abby for this tree?" he asked.

Cheeto laughed. "No, Laddie, I think Abby is with her master's sister. Unfortunately, getting acquainted with her poodles."

"What are poodles?" asked the little tiger.

"Little dogs!" spat Spike. "Sniveling, little, fuzzy, yipping dogs."

"There are little dogs?" asked Flea Biscuit. "As small as me?"

"I think so," said Cheeto. "Although why anyone would want one is beyond me."

Flea Biscuit tried to picture dogs his own size but it was difficult. "They must be very funny to look at," he said, then started to giggle.

"Why yes," added Cheeto, and he began to laugh, too. "I would expect they are."

Spike watched Cheeto and Flea Biscuit laughing, but could not imagine anything about little dogs that would be at all amusing.

The humans continued working on the tree until the sun had nearly set. Finally, they all stood back to admire their work. The man flipped a switch and suddenly the room was filled with a sight more beautiful than the cats had ever seen. There were colored lights, blinking lights, and even bubbling lights. The three friends stared at the tree in awe, the sparkling glow reflected in their wide eyes.

"Wow!" said Flea Biscuit.

"Aye," added Cheeto. "It's the most wonderful thing I've ever seen. What do you think, Spike?"

Spike did not answer. He sat in silence, intently staring up at the glowing star at the top of the tree.

Flea Biscuit thought that Spike looked almost as if he were wishing for something. He turned to Cheeto and whispered, "This is it!"

"What did you say?" asked Cheeto.

"The beginning of the magic," said Flea Biscuit. "This is it. I know it."

Chapter 14

To Flee or Not to, Flea

The humans went into the kitchen, leaving the three cats alone to sit and stare at the sparkling lights. Spike approached the tree and lay down beneath it. Occasionally, he reached up and swatted one of the ornaments to watch the colored lights reflect off of the glass as it swung from side to side. He found sitting beneath this misplaced tree very soothing.

The other two cats soon joined him to explore. Flea Biscuit stared up through the branches but he couldn't see the star at the top. He had a sudden urge to climb to the star. "Could I make it?" he wondered. "Surely the magic must be strongest at the star on the very top. That's what Spike was staring at." He looked at Cheeto and Spike. "They are too big to fit through these branches," he thought, "so it's up to me to make the magic work."

At once, he began squeezing through the branches to get to the magic star high above him. The branches and sharp pine needles scraped against his fur and scratched at his skin, but he continued his mission to the top of the tree.

Seeing the little cat begin to climb, Cheeto called out to him to come down. But he kept climbing.

"Stop!" hissed Spike, but Flea Biscuit did not stop. He was sure he knew what to do. He was going to make everyone happy. He would save Abby from the mean old lady with the poodles and give his humans a new home. He would make everything better.

Cheeto and Spike kept calling for him to come down, but the little tiger ignored them. Decorations fell from the branches, but still he climbed. Beneath the tree, Spike and Cheeto tried to catch the falling ornaments, but there were too many. Some bounced on the floor, but others broke into little pieces.

At last the little tiger neared the top of the tree. He reached out and tried to touch the star, but he wasn't close enough yet. He squeezed his head through the last few branches and stretched his arm as far as it would go. "If I could just touch it!" he thought. He was so close that the light of the star nearly blinded him, but he squinted his eyes and one more time stretched out his paw. At last, he touched the warm golden light of the star. The tree began to sway. Spike and Cheeto dashed out from beneath it. Forward and backward the tree went. Flea Biscuit hung on helplessly as, almost as if time itself had slowed down, the tree came crashing down onto the wooden floor.

Ornaments went popping and rolling across the floor. The star came off the tree and broke into pieces and all of the brightly colored lights went dark. The little girl, the woman, and the man came running into the room.

Cheeto jumped onto the couch and called out, "Flea Biscuit! Where are you? Are you all right?"

Out of the branches squirmed the little tiger, covered in pine needles and scratches but otherwise unharmed.

Spike was furious. He hissed at Flea Biscuit. "Foolish house cat!" he said, then turned and stormed out of the room.

The little girl picked up Flea Biscuit and, after a quick examination, removed the pine needles from his fur. Then she placed him down on the couch beside Cheeto and began to help the woman gather the fallen ornaments off the floor.

The man brought a broom and dustpan and began to sweep up the shards of sparkling glass, tinsel, and pine needles scattered across the floor.

"I'm sorry," Flea Biscuit whispered to Cheeto.

"Now don't you worry about it," said his friend. "The humans don't seem too upset, and I'm sure you won't be doing anything like that ever again."

"No," cried Flea Biscuit as tears began to well up in his eyes. "I'm sorry I ruined the magic. I tried to reach the star and make the magic happen, but instead I've made everything worse."

Cheeto now understood why his friend had so foolishly climbed the tree. "Did you reach the star?" he asked in a kind voice.

"I did!" replied Flea Biscuit. "I touched it, but then I made the tree fall over and now the star is broken and won't ever shine again."

Cheeto could sense how his friend must feel. "It was a noble effort, little one," he said, "and I can't blame you one bit for trying."

But Cheeto could see that, instead of listening, his friend was gazing at the broken star. Then he slumped his shoulders, slid off the couch, and sadly walked out of the room.

"Don't worry your little head!" Cheeto called out as he hopped into one of the empty boxes on the floor. "I'll stay here and supervise the cleanup."

Flea Biscuit didn't hear him. He headed upstairs to hide under the little girl's bed.

Chapter 15

Silent Night

Although Spike was still angry with Flea Biscuit, he had other concerns. He retreated to the kitchen and sat by the sliding glass door to watch the back porch and see if his friend the possum would come for dinner. Left and right his green eyes scanned the trees for movement. He cursed as a light snow again began to fall.

Beneath the little girl's bed, Flea Biscuit was cold and sad. Above him he could hear the woman tucking the little girl in under the blankets. He felt as though he had ruined the magic for everyone.

As the woman walked out, she partly closed the door and turned off the lights, leaving the room dark except for a small night light in the corner. A moment later he heard the girl moving above him. Suddenly her head was upside down, looking under the bed at him. She smiled, hopped out from under the blankets and reached to pull him out. He struggled at first, but relented when he realized how good it would feel to receive a little hug from her. She got back into bed and curled her arms around Flea Biscuit to let him know that she still loved him. He began to purr and soon they were both asleep.

In the kitchen, Spike watched the man and woman share a glass of wine. Then he turned back to the sliding glass door, still hoping to see his friend the possum. After a while, he laid down beside the door and watched the snow softly cover the porch. Slowly, he closed his eyes.

In the room with the fireplace, Cheeto was curled up in the empty box. He had watched as the humans rebuilt the tree as best they could. The woman gave him a pat on the head as they left him alone there for the night. With the tree standing again, the fire dying down, and the day's activities over, he drifted off to sleep in the darkening room.

He was snoring loudly and did not waken when, much later, someone came into the room and quietly began repairing the strings of colored lights and placing pretty boxes under the tree.

Flea Biscuit's Magic Christmas

Chapter 16

A Magic Day

The sound of the man placing wood into the fireplace awoke Cheeto from his deep sleep. He squinted his eyes and yawned as he sat up in his box on the floor. Suddenly his eyes grew wide as he saw that beneath the tree were many other boxes, all wrapped in pretty paper tied with ribbons and bows he wanted to play with. He then noticed that the tree was lit up again. It looked as bright and magical as ever! Even the broken star was repaired and glowing atop the tree!

"I must tell Flea Biscuit!" he thought. "The magic is real!" He quickly hopped out of his box and ran up the stairs to the little girl's room. He jumped up on the bed, waking the girl and the little tiger.

Flea Biscuit yawned and slowly opened his eyes. "Cheeto, what's going on? Why are you so happy?"

Cheeto was prancing in a circle excitedly. He playfully tapped the little tiger on the nose. "You must come and see!" He was panting with excitement. "The magic!"

Flea Biscuit jumped from the bed. The little girl grabbed her robe and followed the two cats down the stairs into the room with the fireplace. There, they gazed upon the tree, which now appeared even brighter and more beautiful than it had been before.

Hearing the excitement, Spike awoke. His muscles were sore from sleeping on the cold kitchen floor all night. He squinted as he looked out onto the back porch. The sun was shining brightly and it looked as if the day would be warmer. However, the bowl of food left for his friend remained frozen and untouched, dusted with a fine layer of snow. Spike let out a sigh.

Suddenly, Cheeto came bounding up to him. "Spike! Spike!" he called.

"What is it?" said Spike, annoyed at so much noise this early in his day.

"Come and see!" said Cheeto. "The magic! Come and see!"

Spike groaned as he stood up, stretched, and then followed Cheeto down the hall to the room with the fireplace. There stood the tree, shining and bright, and underneath were packages with ribbons and bows. Spike, too, was taken aback by the sight. "Well, clearly," he said, "the man must have repaired everything last night while we slept."

"No," said Cheeto. I was here in this room all night and saw nothing. I am certain that this is the magic of the season we were hoping for!"

"I'm so excited!" added Flea Biscuit as he ran left and right and between the neatly wrapped packages. "What's in these pretty boxes?"

Spike walked closer to the tree to examine it. He looked from the bright star down to the lowest branches covered with lights and shining ornaments. He squinted his green eyes suspiciously. In spite of the damage from the previous night, the tree was as stunning as it had ever been. "Hmmm," he said. "It certainly looks beautiful, but I don't know if it's magic. I will need further proof."

"Oh, Spike," said Cheeto. "Ever suspicious of a happy turn of events."

"Proof!" Spike said defiantly.

Then, as if on cue, the doorbell rang. The man went to answer it and the cats followed. There in the doorway stood an old woman. In her hand was a leash, and on the end of that leash was Abby.

Chapter 17

Welcome Home

The man invited the woman inside but she refused. She seemed angry with Abby. Finally, she tossed the man Abby's leash, turned, and walked back to her car in a huff. Abby's eyes followed her uncertainly, but the man commanded her to stay. In response, the golden retriever smiled and wagged her tail. Then the man knelt down to Abby, whispered a few words and with a pat on her head and a quick whistle he commanded her to come inside the house. With that, Abby realized that the man was her new master and this was to be her new home.

She walked out of the cold and into the house, where she met the cats. At once, she began licking them. "Abby," giggled Flea, "are you going to stay here now?"

"Yes!" she said excitedly.

Before Abby could lick him, Spike stepped back and let out a howl in protest. "Now I have to share the house with a dog?" He hissed at Cheeto. "So much for your magic!"

The orange tabby paid no attention to Spike. He knew that Abby's arrival was indeed a magical thing. "Tell us what happened!" he said excitedly.

"Well," replied Abby, "I tried to get along with my new mistress' poodles, but they are not very nice dogs and are simply terrible at playing tag and chase. I ran all over the house with them but they just kept hiding behind my mistress and barking at me. I guess I was trying too hard to be their friend, but anyway, my mistress got so angry that she brought me to the shelter even though the man had told her he would adopt me."

Abby said it all so quickly that the cats had trouble understanding every word, but they understood enough to nod along with the story.

"That spiteful woman," Cheeto added.

"So, how did you end up here and not at the shelter?" asked Flea Biscuit.

Abby continued, "Well, for some reason the shelter was closed today! So, my mistress gave up and drove me all the way back here. Since your man accepted me, he is my new master just like with you."

"The man is not my master!" said Spike angrily. "I work for the man and he feeds me and allows me to stay."

"Now, Spike," chided Cheeto, "haven't we been over that enough?"

Realizing the dog must finally be finished with her story, Flea Biscuit let out a loud and happy, "Welcome to your forever home, Abby!"

Spike groaned, but no one was listening. They were all distracted by the sound of tearing paper and laughter coming from the room with the fireplace.

"More magic!" said Flea Biscuit excitedly. The four pets hurried into the room to see what was happening.

The little girl was opening a large box. From inside, she slowly slid out what appeared to be a miniature version of the man's home.

"Well, I'll be!" said Cheeto.

"It looks like this house," exclaimed Flea Biscuit, "but why is it so small? Will mice live in there?"

Spike swatted at the little tiger's head. "Never!" Spike hissed. "Could this day get any worse?" he thought. "I now have to live with a dog, and the man has built a house for mice!"

Cheeto happily walked around the little house, examining every detail. Inside were miniature models of the three humans and of himself, Spike, and Flea Biscuit. "Come see!" he meowed. "There are little versions of all of us inside!"

"Let me see!" cried Abby. She spun her tail so excitedly that she nearly knocked the little home over.

"Oh, it is a toy," said Spike relieved.

Flea Biscuit laughed as he tried to reach inside to catch the humans.

The little girl thanked the man for the gift, but her face looked somewhat confused. It was then that the man took out a small, exquisitely wrapped little box and gave it to the woman. As she opened it, she began to cry. The four friends had never seen a human crying because of a little box. But then the woman took from the box a gold ring with one bright stone. She smiled through her tears as she slipped on the ring and then held her hand in the light from the window. From the stone, all the colors of a rainbow shone across the room.

This was something Cheeto thought must be a very magical thing for humans. Possibly the most powerful magic of all. "Look!" he whispered to Flea Biscuit.

"It's beautiful!" Flea Biscuit whispered back, "but what does it mean?"

"I think it means that now we are all going to be together forever," Cheeto replied.

"Well," said Abby, "allow me to return the sentiment, little tiger. Welcome to your forever home!"

Flea Biscuit's Magic Christmas

Chapter 18

The Magic of Family

Everyone was happy… except Spike. The black cat quietly slinked out of the room and went upstairs to be alone. His world was changing so quickly, and he was, at heart, a solitary animal. He felt as if he would no longer fit in at the big old house. He ventured into the man's bedroom, a place he rarely entered, and crawled onto the bed. He laid his head down by the man's pillow and let out a sigh. "Is this no longer where I will live?" he thought. "The man has Cheeto and Abby to hunt for him now. Who will appreciate my work?" He closed his eyes. "This is not magic," he thought.

Hours passed. Spike drifted in and out of sleep. When he was awake, he could hear the celebrating downstairs, but he had no desire to take part in it. Then, as the afternoon sunlight streamed through a window and warmed his fur, he woke to the sound of little footsteps entering the room. He opened his eyes.

Flea Biscuit, concerned for his housemate, had decided to go and look for Spike. He was still wary of the moody black cat, but his concerns overruled his fear.

He climbed onto the bed very slowly. "What's wrong, Sir?" he asked in a timid voice.

"Nothing," said Spike. "I just want to be alone."

"Don't you want to be with your family?" Flea Biscuit asked.

"Family?" Spike thought. The very word pulled at his heart. "Is that what we are?" Spike raised his head and asked Flea Biscuit: "We are a family?"

"Why, yes, of course we are," said the little tiger. "You, Cheeto, Abby, me, and of course our humans. You now have three humans of your own Spike. It's magic!"

Magic or not, Spike tried to imagine what life in a family would be like. He thought back to the days when it was just him and the man in the house. "Was it better then?" he considered. "No, it was different, but not necessarily better. Perhaps I have a place in this family after all."

The face of an orange tabby poked up over the side of the bed. "Hey, do you smell that?" He took a long sniff. "Oh, it's such a wonderful aroma. Do you know what it is? Abby says the woman is cooking the large bird that the old farmer had given to the man. Come down and see. Perhaps they will give us a taste."

"Come on, Spike," said Flea Biscuit. "Come and be with your family."

The three cats went down the back stairway to the kitchen. There, they sat patiently for what seemed like hours as the man and woman finished preparing the meal.

Just before dinner was to be served, the man set up a camera in the room by the Christmas tree, and the three humans gathered all of the animals with them to pose for a photograph. The little girl held Flea Biscuit. Abby sat proudly by the man's feet. The woman scooped up Cheeto and hugged him. "She has chosen to be my own human!" he thought, and began to purr.

The only one missing was Spike. He sat by the camera stand, watching the scene.

The man walked over, hit a button on the camera, then quickly picked up the slim black cat and returned to his place for the photo. Spike squirmed and clawed, but the man held him tight. There was a bright flash, and then the man finally let go of him.

Spike sprinted out of the room and returned to the kitchen, wondering what had just happened. "Obviously more magic I don't need," he thought, but his mood quickly changed as the oven door was opened and the wonderful scent of roasted turkey filled the room.

At last, dinner was ready. The man cut the turkey into thin slices and put them on a large platter, which he placed on the table along with the rest of the feast. Then he placed four small bowls of turkey in front of the pets. "Yum!" said Cheeto as he took a long deep breath of the scent.

Before the cats had even taken a bite, Abby had finished her turkey and was looking to see if she could get another serving. "That was my bird," she said. "My master and I caught that bird."

"And it is delicious!" added Cheeto as he slowly chewed.

"Yes, thank you, Abby," added Flea Biscuit.

Spike carried his portion away to enjoy by the lights of the tree.

At the table, the humans said a prayer, raised their glasses, and toasted the old farmer who had provided them all with the wonderful meal. The man praised his friend's kind heart, and vowed to always be a good master to his beloved dog.

Flea Biscuit sat up and smiled. Everyone in his family had gotten something very special this day. Including Spike, even if he might not understand it yet. As he looked at all the happy faces, he said one simple word. "Magic."

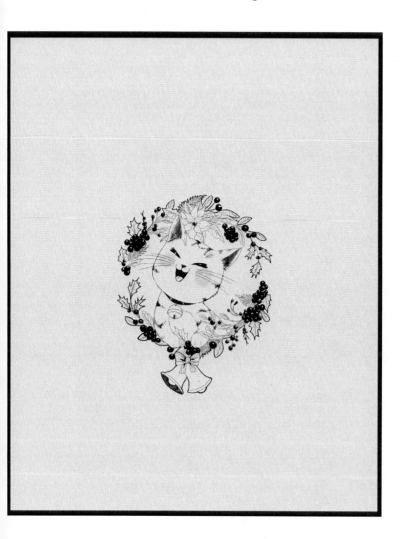

Chapter 19

One Last Look

It had been an exciting but exhausting day at the big old house. Much had happened and, in many ways, all of their lives had changed.

In the dark, Spike sat alone on the back porch and waited, hoping for one last bit of magic to occur. The winter wind blew on his fur and whiskers as he sat and waited, looking left and right through the trees. He took a deep breath of the cold night air, then exhaled, watching as the vapor from his breath disappeared.

"Perhaps we have used up all of the magic," he thought. Still, he waited.

Behind him, the glass door slid open. Cheeto slipped out of the warmth to join his friend. "Any sign of him?" he asked.

"Not yet," Spike replied softly.

Cheeto sat close to Spike. After a long pause, he said, "Life is a funny thing, you know, Spike? Why, just last winter I was out there huddled in my burrow, trying to stay warm, and now, look at what has happened. I've got a home, friends, and even a family. It's because of you, Spike. You rescued me when I was wounded and hiding in my burrow. I have not forgotten that you are a true friend."

Spike replied with a barely audible, "Sure."

"Do not be hard on yourself, no matter what comes your way," Cheeto added. "You are a good cat, and the possum, wherever he may be, had a loyal friend and protector in this life, and that's the most magical gift anyone can ever hope for."

Spike shifted and braced against the cold wind. "Thank you," he said. Slowly, he raised his head, looked up at the brightest star in the sky, and wished as hard as he could to hear that low, soft squeak from his friend in the woods.

The End

WRITE TO THE AUTHOR

Do you have a cat or other pet? I'd love to hear your story.

You can contact me or my pets at:

MBonazzoli@gmail.com

Visit Flea Biscuit and Friends on the web at www.FleaBiscuit.com

Made in United States
North Haven, CT
10 November 2021

11009784R00058